ADAPTED BY

RICHARD APPIGNANESI

ILLUSTRATED BY

NANA LI

Amulet Books, New York

PUBLISHER'S NOTE: This is a work of fiction. Names, characters, places, and incidents are either the product of the author's imagination or are used fictitiously, and any resemblance to actual persons, living or dead, business establishments, events, or locales is entirely coincidental.

Library of Congress Cataloging-in-Publication Data

Appignanesi, Richard.
Twelfth night / by William Shakespeare ; adapted by Richard Appignanesi.
p. cm. — (Manga Shakespeare)
Summary: Retells, in comic book format, Shakespeare's comedy about Viola who, upon finding herself shipwrecked, pretends to be a servant but finds herself falling in love with Duke Orsino.
ISBN 978-0-8109-9718-9 (alk. paper)
1. Graphic novels. [1. Graphic novels. 2. Shakespeare, William, 1564–1616. Twelfth night.—Adaptations.] I. Shakespeare, William, 1564–1616. Twelfth night. II. Title.
PZ7.7.A67Twe 2011
741.5'941—dc22
2010024429

Originally published in the U.K. by SelfMadeHero
(www.selfmadehero.com)

Illustrator: Nana Li
Text Adaptor: Richard Appignanesi
Designer: Andy Huckle
Textual Consultant: Nick de Somogyi
Publisher: Emma Hayley

Printed and bound in China
10 9 8 7 6

Amulet Books are available at special discounts when purchased in quantity for premiums and promotions as well as fundraising or educational use. Special editions can also be created to specification. For details, contact specialsales@abramsbooks.com or the address below.

ABRAMS The Art of Books
195 Broadway, New York, NY 10007
abramsbooks.com

Viola (later disguised as the page-boy Cesario)
"Disguise, I see thou art a wickedness!"
Sebastian, her twin brother
"If it be thus to dream, still let me sleep!"
"One face, one voice, one habit – and two persons!"

Countess Olivia of Illyria, in mourning for her brother
"We will draw the curtain and show you the picture..."
"If music be the food of love, play on!"
Duke Orsino of Illyria, in love with Olivia

Sir Andrew Aguecheek, a foolish gentleman
"Shall we set about some revels?"
"A plague on these pickle-herring!"
Sir Toby Belch, Olivia's drunken cousin

Malvolio, Olivia's butler

"I'll be revenged on the whole pack of you!"

Maria, Olivia's maidservant

"What a caterwauling do you keep here!"

A Sea-Captain
"This is Illyria, lady..."
Antonio, Sebastian's friend and protector
"His life I gave him, and did thereto add my love..."

Feste, the Fool in Olivia's household
"Many a good hanging prevents a bad marriage!"
"Sportful malice may pluck on laughter!"
Fabian, a servant in Olivia's household

Curio, a servant to Orsino
"Will you go hunt the hart?"
Valentine, another servant to Orsino
"If the Duke continue these favours..."
A Priest of Illyria
"A contract of eternal bond of love!"

A shipwreck off the coast of Illyria...

IF MUSIC BE THE FOOD OF LOVE, PLAY ON,
GIVE ME EXCESS OF IT, THAT THE APPETITE MAY SICKEN AND SO DIE.
ENOUGH! NO MORE!
'TIS NOT SO SWEET NOW AS IT WAS BEFORE.

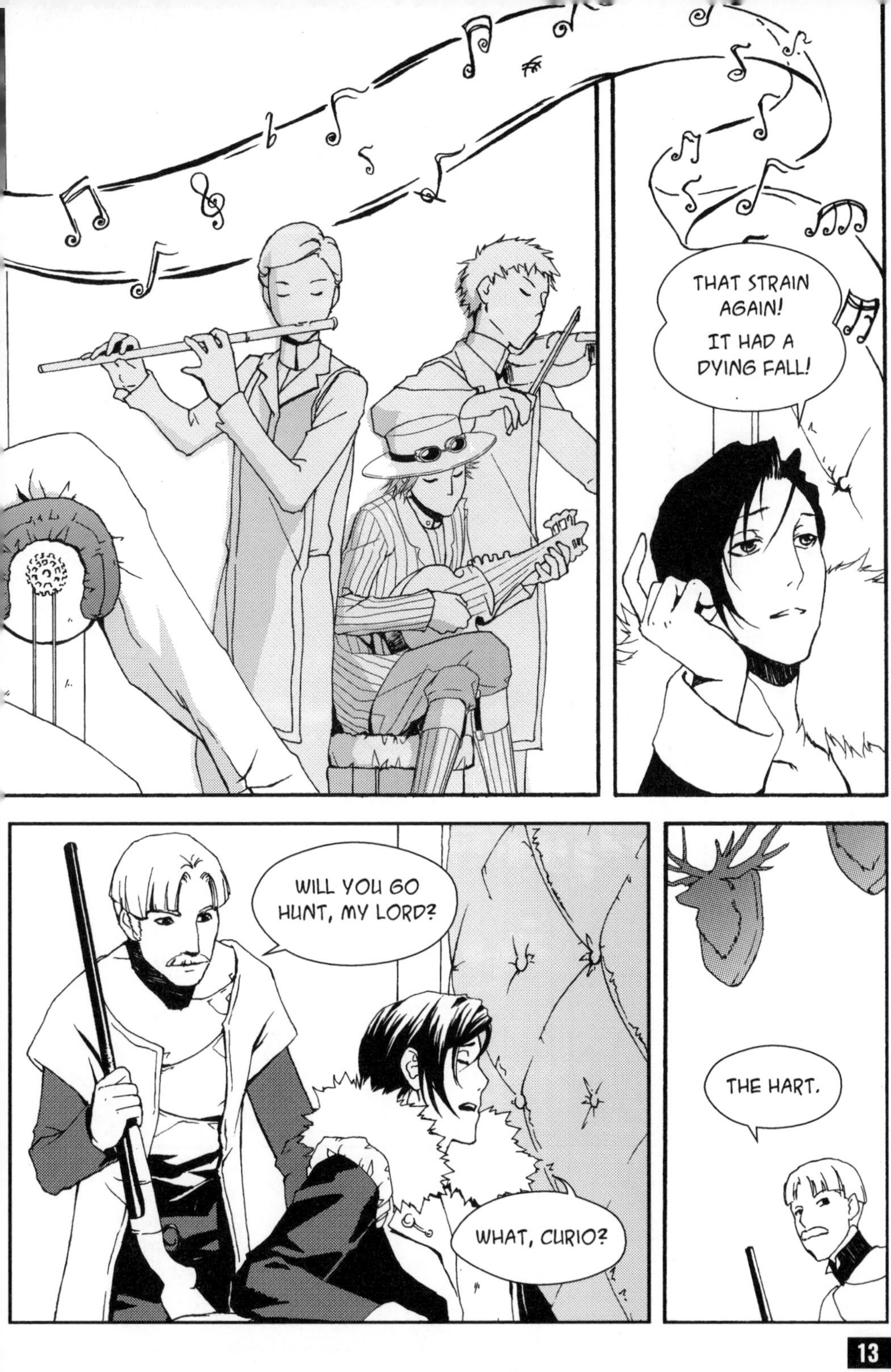

THAT STRAIN AGAIN!
IT HAD A DYING FALL!

WHY, SO I DO, THE NOBLEST THAT I HAVE.
O, WHEN MINE EYES DID SEE OLIVIA FIRST, THAT INSTANT WAS I TURNED INTO A HART...
AND MY DESIRES, LIKE CRUEL HOUNDS, EVER SINCE PURSUE ME.
HOW NOW!
WHAT NEWS FROM HER?
I FROM HER HANDMAID DO RETURN THIS ANSWER.

THE ELEMENT ITSELF, TILL SEVEN YEARS, SHALL NOT BEHOLD HER FACE...
BUT LIKE A CLOISTRESS SHE WILL VEILÈD WALK,
AND WATER ONCE A DAY HER CHAMBER ROUND WITH EYE-OFFENDING BRINE.
ALL THIS TO SEASON A BROTHER'S DEAD LOVE,
WHICH SHE WOULD KEEP LASTING IN HER SAD REMEMBRANCE.

O, SHE THAT HATH A HEART TO PAY THIS DEBT OF LOVE BUT TO A BROTHER...
FWMP
HOW WILL SHE LOVE WHEN LIVER, BRAIN AND HEART...
ARE ALL SUPPLIED AND FILLED...
WITH ONE SELF KING!

AWAY BEFORE ME TO SWEET BEDS OF FLOWERS.
LOVE THOUGHTS LIE RICH WHEN CANOPIED WITH BOWERS.

WHAT COUNTRY, FRIENDS, IS THIS?
THIS IS ILLYRIA, LADY.
AND WHAT SHOULD I DO IN ILLYRIA?
MY BROTHER IS IN ELYSIUM. PERCHANCE HE IS NOT DROWNED.
WHAT THINK YOU, SAILORS?
IT IS PERCHANCE THAT YOU YOURSELF WERE SAVED.

O MY POOR BROTHER!
AND SO PERCHANCE MAY HE BE.
TRUE, MADAM.
AFTER OUR SHIP DID SPLIT, I SAW YOUR BROTHER BIND HIMSELF TO A STRONG MAST, WHERE I SAW HIM HOLD, SO LONG AS I COULD SEE.

FOR SAYING SO, THERE'S GOLD!
KNOW'ST THOU THIS COUNTRY?
AY, MADAM, WELL, FOR I WAS BRED AND BORN NOT THREE HOURS FROM THIS VERY PLACE.
WHO GOVERNS HERE?
A NOBLE DUKE, ORSINO.

ORSINO!
HAVE HEARD MY FATHER NAME HIM.
HE WAS A BACHELOR THEN.
AND SO IS NOW, FOR BUT A MONTH AGO I WENT FROM HENCE...
AND THEN 'TWAS FRESH IN MURMUR THAT HE DID SEEK THE LOVE OF FAIR OLIVIA.
NOD
WHAT'S SHE?
THE DAUGHTER OF A COUNT THAT DIED, THEN LEAVING HER IN THE PROTECTION OF HER BROTHER, WHO SHORTLY ALSO DIED...
FOR WHOSE DEAR LOVE, THEY SAY, SHE HATH ABJURED THE SIGHT AND COMPANY OF MEN.

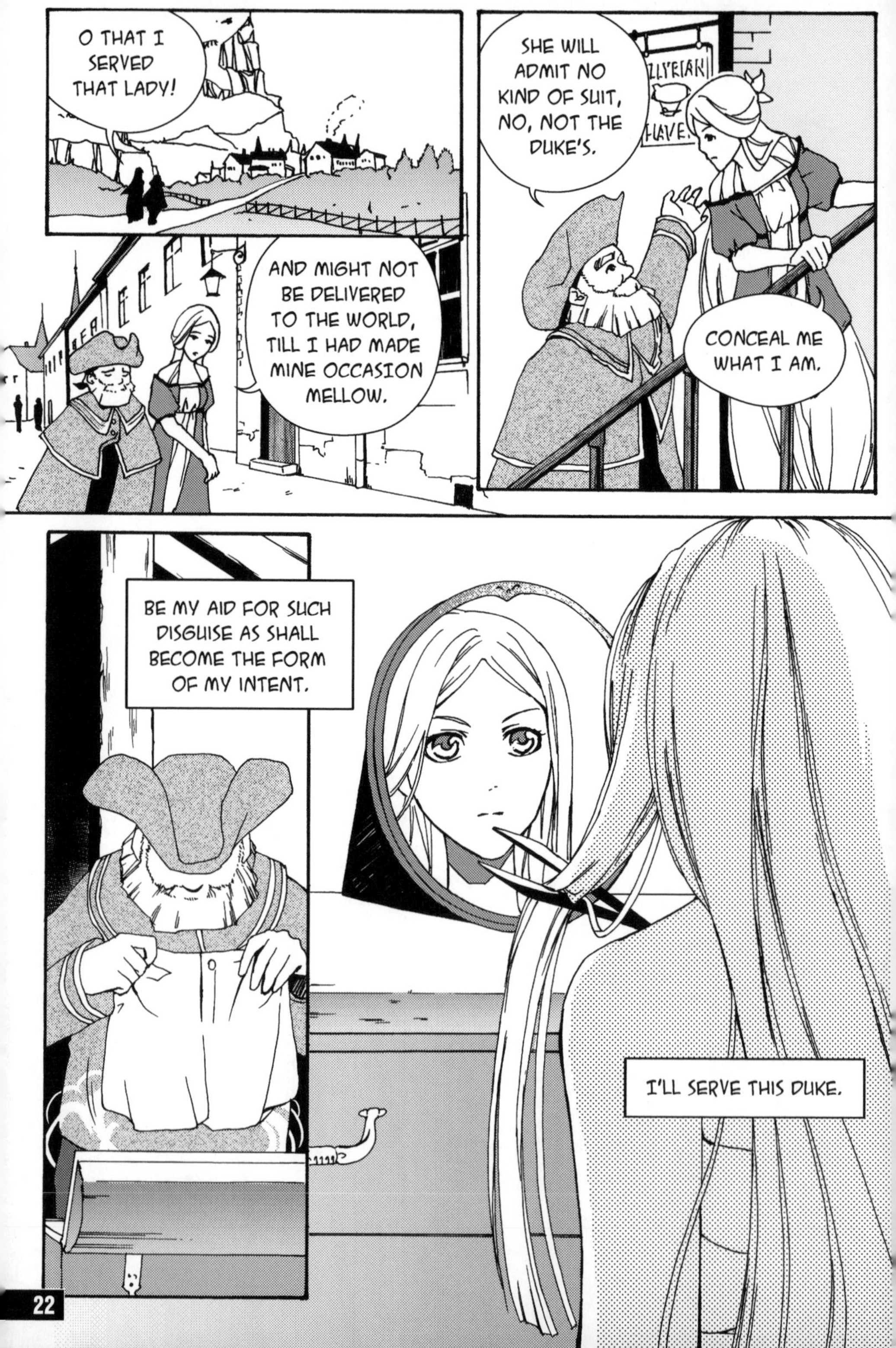
O THAT I SERVED THAT LADY!
SHE WILL ADMIT NO KIND OF SUIT, NO, NOT THE DUKE'S.
AND MIGHT NOT BE DELIVERED TO THE WORLD, TILL I HAD MADE MINE OCCASION MELLOW.
CONCEAL ME WHAT I AM.
BE MY AID FOR SUCH DISGUISE AS SHALL BECOME THE FORM OF MY INTENT.
I'LL SERVE THIS DUKE.

WHAT ELSE MAY HAP TO TIME I WILL COMMIT.
ONLY SHAPE THY SILENCE TO MY WIT.
YOUR MUTE I'LL BE.
WHEN MY TONGUE BLABS, THEN LET MINE EYES NOT SEE.
LEAD ME ON.

CHIRP
CHIRP
WHAT A PLAGUE MEANS MY NIECE TO TAKE THE DEATH OF HER BROTHER THUS?
TWEET
SIR TOBY, YOU MUST COME IN EARLIER AT NIGHTS.
MY LADY TAKES GREAT EXCEPTIONS TO YOUR ILL HOURS.
YOU MUST CONFINE YOURSELF WITHIN THE MODEST LIMITS OF ORDER.
CONFINE?
I'LL CONFINE MYSELF NO FINER THAN I AM.

THAT QUAFFING AND DRINKING WILL UNDO YOU.
OW OW OW OW
I HEARD MY LADY TALK OF A FOOLISH KNIGHT THAT YOU BROUGHT IN HERE TO BE HER WOOER.
WOBBLE
WHO? SIR ANDREW AGUECHEEK?
WOBBLE
SIGH
AY, HE.
WHY, HE HAS THREE THOUSAND DUCATS A YEAR.

BUT HE'LL HAVE BUT A YEAR IN ALL THESE DUCATS.
HE'S A FOOL AND A PRODIGAL.
HE PLAYS THE VIOL-DE-GAMBA AND SPEAKS THREE OR FOUR LANGUAGES.
BESIDES THAT HE'S A FOOL,
A GREAT QUARRELLER
AND A COWARD.
THEY ARE SCOUNDRELS THAT SAY SO OF HIM!
SPLOSH

CLANK

POP

POP

POP

BLINK

BLINK

MOREOVER, HE'S DRUNK NIGHTLY IN YOUR COMPANY.

PAT

PAT

WITH DRINKING HEALTHS TO MY NIECE.

I'LL DRINK TO HER AS LONG AS THERE IS A PASSAGE IN MY THROAT AND DRINK IN ILLYRIA.

HOW NOW, SIR TOBY BELCH!
SLAP
BLESS YOU, FAIR SHREW.
ACCOST, SIR ANDREW, ACCOST!
MY NIECE'S CHAMBERMAID.
GOOD MISTRESS ACCOST, I DESIRE BETTER ACQUAINTANCE.
MY NAME IS MARY, SIR.
GOOD MISTRESS MARY ACCOST –

YOU MISTAKE, KNIGHT.
"ACCOST" IS, FRONT HER...
BOARD HER...
WOO HER...
ASSAIL HER!
IS THAT THE MEANING OF "ACCOST"?
O KNIGHT, WHEN DID I SEE THEE SO PUT DOWN?
NEVER IN YOUR LIFE.
FAIR LADY, DO YOU THINK YOU HAVE FOOLS IN HAND?
SIR, I HAVE NOT YOU BY THE HAND.
METHINKS SOMETIMES I HAVE NO MORE WIT THAN AN ORDINARY MAN HAS.

I'LL HOME TOMORROW, SIR TOBY.
YOUR NIECE WILL NOT BE SEEN, OR, IF SHE BE, SHE'LL NONE OF ME.
THE COUNT HIMSELF WOOS HER.
SHE'LL NONE OF THE COUNT.
SHE'LL NOT MATCH ABOVE HER DEGREE, NEITHER IN ESTATE, YEARS NOR WIT.
I HAVE HEARD HER SWEAR IT.

I'LL STAY A MONTH LONGER.
I AM A FELLOW OF THE STRANGEST MIND IN THE WORLD.
I DELIGHT IN REVELS SOMETIMES ALTOGETHER.
WHAT IS THY EXCELLENCE IN A GALLIARD, KNIGHT?
FAITH, I CAN CUT A CAPER.

WHEREFORE ARE THESE THINGS HID?
IS IT A WORLD TO HIDE VIRTUES IN?
I DID THINK, BY THE EXCELLENT CONSTITUTION OF THY LEG, IT WAS FORMED UNDER THE STAR OF A GALLIARD.
AY, 'TIS STRONG.
SHALL WE SET ABOUT SOME REVELS?
WHAT SHALL WE DO ELSE?
WERE WE NOT BORN UNDER TAURUS?

TAURUS? THAT'S SIDES AND HEART.
NO, SIR. IT IS LEGS AND THIGHS.
LET ME SEE THEE CAPER.
HA! HIGHER!
KLACK
EXCELLENT!
HAHAHA!
HAHA!
FWIP
SPLASH

IF THE DUKE CONTINUE THESE FAVOURS TOWARDS YOU, CESARIO, YOU ARE LIKE TO BE MUCH ADVANCED.
HE HATH KNOWN YOU BUT THREE DAYS, AND ALREADY YOU ARE NO STRANGER.
IS HE INCONSTANT, SIR, IN HIS FAVOURS?
NO, BELIEVE ME.
I THANK YOU.
HERE COMES THE COUNT.

CESARIO, THOU KNOW'ST NO LESS BUT ALL.
I HAVE UNCLASPED TO THEE THE BOOK EVEN OF MY SECRET SOUL.
THEREFORE, GOOD YOUTH, ADDRESS THY GAIT UNTO HER.
BE NOT DENIED ACCESS.
STAND AT HER DOORS TILL THOU HAVE AUDIENCE.

SAY I DO SPEAK WITH HER, MY LORD —
WHAT THEN?
O, THEN UNFOLD THE PASSION OF MY LOVE.
SURPRISE HER WITH DISCOURSE OF MY DEAR FAITH.
SHE WILL ATTEND IT BETTER IN THY YOUTH.
I THINK NOT SO, MY LORD.
DEAR LAD, BELIEVE IT.
FOR THEY SHALL BELIE THY YEARS THAT SAY THOU ART A MAN.

THY SMALL PIPE IS AS THE MAIDEN'S ORGAN.
AND ALL IS SEMBLATIVE A WOMAN'S PART.
GULP
DIANA'S LIP IS NOT MORE SMOOTH.
PROSPER WELL IN THIS, AND THOU SHALT LIVE AS FREELY AS THY LORD, TO CALL HIS FORTUNES THINE.
I'LL DO MY BEST TO WOO YOUR LADY.
SIGH
YET, WHOEVER I WOO, MYSELF WOULD BE HIS WIFE.
SIGH

CRASH
MY LADY WILL HANG THEE FOR THY ABSENCE.
LET HER! MANY A GOOD HANGING PREVENTS A BAD MARRIAGE.
YOU ARE RESOLUTE, THEN?
I AM RESOLVED ON TWO POINTS.

THAT IF ONE BREAK, THE OTHER WILL HOLD.
OR IF BOTH BREAK, YOUR GASKINS FALL.
VERY APT!
IF SIR TOBY WOULD LEAVE DRINKING, THOU WERT AS WITTY A PIECE OF EVE'S FLESH AS ANY IN ILLYRIA.
SNAP
HERE COMES MY LADY.
MAKE YOUR EXCUSE WISELY, YOU WERE BEST.
SLAM

GOD BLESS THEE, LADY!
TAKE THE FOOL AWAY.
DO YOU NOT HEAR, FELLOWS? TAKE AWAY THE LADY.
SIR, I BADE THEM TAKE AWAY YOU.
MISPRISION IN THE HIGHEST DEGREE!
GOOD MADONNA, GIVE ME LEAVE TO PROVE YOU A FOOL.

CAN YOU DO IT?
MAKE YOUR PROOF.
DEXTERIOUSLY, MADONNA.
WHY MOURN'ST THOU?
GOOD FOOL, FOR MY BROTHER'S DEATH.
CLENCH
I THINK HIS SOUL IS IN HELL, MADONNA.

I KNOW HIS SOUL IS IN HEAVEN, FOOL.
THE MORE FOOL YOU TO MOURN FOR YOUR BROTHER'S SOUL, BEING IN HEAVEN.
TAKE AWAY THE FOOL, GENTLEMEN.
WHAT THINK YOU OF THIS FOOL, MALVOLIO?
I MARVEL YOUR LADYSHIP TAKES DELIGHT IN SUCH A BARREN RASCAL.
I SAW HIM PUT DOWN THE OTHER DAY WITH AN ORDINARY FOOL THAT HAS NO MORE BRAIN THAN A STONE.

LOOK YOU NOW – HE'S OUT OF HIS GUARD ALREADY.
BLEH
O, YOU ARE SICK OF SELF-LOVE, MALVOLIO, AND TASTE WITH A DISTEMPERED APPETITE.
THERE IS NO SLANDER IN AN ALLOWED FOOL.
THERE IS AT THE GATE A YOUNG GENTLEMAN DESIRES TO SPEAK WITH YOU.

FROM THE COUNT ORSINO, IS IT?
I KNOW NOT, MADAM.
'TIS A FAIR YOUNG MAN.
PING
GO YOU, MALVOLIO.
IF IT BE A SUIT FROM THE COUNT, I AM SICK, OR NOT AT HOME –
WHAT YOU WILL TO DISMISS IT.
BOW

NOW YOU SEE, SIR, HOW YOUR FOOLING GROWS OLD, AND PEOPLE DISLIKE IT.
THOU HAST SPOKE FOR US, MADONNA, FOR HERE COMES...
ONE OF THY KIN.
SHUFFLE
SHUFFLE
HALF DRUNK!
BURP!
POP
POP
A PLAGUE ON THESE PICKLE-HERRING!
COUSIN, HOW HAVE YOU COME SO EARLY BY THIS LETHARGY?
"LECHERY"?
I DEFY LECHERY.
SMACK
THERE'S ONE AT THE GATE.
AY, MARRY, WHAT IS HE?
LET HIM BE THE DEVIL, I CARE NOT!

WHAT'S A DRUNKEN MAN LIKE, FOOL?
LIKE A DROWNED MAN, A FOOL, AND A MADMAN.
ONE DRAUGHT MAKES HIM A FOOL...
THE SECOND MADS HIM...
AND A THIRD DROWNS HIM.
HE'S IN THE THIRD DEGREE OF DRINK.
HE'S DROWNED. GO, LOOK AFTER HIM.
RA RA
RA RA
RA
HE IS BUT MAD YET, MADONNA...
AND THE FOOL SHALL LOOK TO THE MADMAN.
KSHH
KSHH
CLOSE

MADAM, YOND YOUNG FELLOW SWEARS HE WILL SPEAK WITH YOU.
WHAT IS TO BE SAID TO HIM, LADY? HE'S FORTIFIED AGAINST ANY DENIAL.
TELL HIM HE SHALL NOT SPEAK WITH ME.
HAS BEEN TOLD SO, AND HE SAYS HE'LL STAND AT YOUR DOOR LIKE A POST.
WHAT KIND OF MAN IS HE?

NOT YET OLD ENOUGH FOR A MAN, NOR YOUNG ENOUGH FOR A BOY.
ONE WOULD THINK HIS MOTHER'S MILK WERE SCARCE OUT OF HIM.
LET HIM APPROACH.
POFF
CALL IN MY GENTLEWOMAN.
GIVE ME MY VEIL.
COME, THROW IT OVER MY FACE.
SIGH
WE'LL ONCE MORE HEAR ORSINO'S EMBASSY.

THE HONOURABLE LADY OF THE HOUSE...
WHICH IS SHE?
SPEAK TO ME. I SHALL ANSWER FOR HER.
MOST RADIANT, EXQUISITE, AND UNMATCHABLE BEAUTY –
GOOD GENTLE ONE, GIVE ME MODEST ASSURANCE IF YOU BE THE LADY OF THE HOUSE, THAT I MAY PROCEED IN MY SPEECH.
ARE YOU A COMEDIAN?

NO, MY PROFOUND HEART. YET, I SWEAR, I AM NOT THAT I PLAY.
ARE YOU THE LADY OF THE HOUSE?
IF I DO NOT USURP MYSELF, I AM.
MOST CERTAIN, IF YOU ARE SHE, YOU DO USURP YOURSELF.
FOR WHAT IS YOURS TO BESTOW IS NOT YOURS TO RESERVE.

I HEARD YOU WERE SAUCY AT MY GATES.
IF YOU BE NOT MAD, BE GONE.
IF YOU HAVE REASON, BE BRIEF.
WILL YOU HOIST SAIL, SIR?
HERE LIES YOUR WAY.
NO, I AM TO HULL HERE A LITTLE LONGER.
SPEAK YOUR OFFICE.

IT ALONE CONCERNS YOUR EAR.
YET YOU BEGAN RUDELY.
WHAT ARE YOU?
WHAT I AM AND WHAT I WOULD ARE AS SECRET AS MAIDENHEAD —
TO YOUR EARS, DIVINITY, TO ANY OTHER'S, PROFANATION.
GIVE US THE PLACE ALONE.
CLICK

NOW, SIR, WHERE LIES YOUR TEXT?
IN ORSINO'S BOSOM.
SIGH
O, I HAVE READ IT. IT IS HERESY.
HAVE YOU NO MORE TO SAY?
GOOD MADAM, LET ME SEE YOUR FACE.

BUT WE WILL DRAW THE CURTAIN AND SHOW YOU THE PICTURE.
YOU ARE NOW OUT OF YOUR TEXT.
LOOK YOU, SIR.
IS IT NOT WELL DONE?
LADY, YOU ARE THE CRUELLEST SHE ALIVE IF YOU WILL LEAD THESE GRACES TO THE GRAVE, AND LEAVE THE WORLD NO COPY.

IT SHALL BE INVENTORIED AS...
ITEM:
TWO LIPS, INDIFFERENT RED.
ITEM:
TWO GREY EYES, WITH LIDS TO THEM.
ITEM:
ONE NECK,
ONE CHIN,
AND SO FORTH.
WERE YOU SENT HITHER TO PRAISE ME?
I SEE YOU WHAT YOU ARE.
YOU ARE TOO PROUD.
BUT, IF YOU WERE THE DEVIL, YOU ARE FAIR.

MY LORD LOVES YOU.
O, SUCH LOVE COULD BE BUT RECOMPENSED THOUGH YOU WERE CROWNED THE NONPAREIL OF BEAUTY!
HOW DOES HE LOVE ME?
WITH ADORATIONS, FERTILE TEARS,
WITH GROANS THAT THUNDER LOVE,
WITH SIGHS OF FIRE.
YOUR LORD DOES KNOW MY MIND.
I CANNOT LOVE HIM.

YET I KNOW HIM NOBLE, OF GREAT ESTATE, OF STAINLESS YOUTH, FREE, LEARNED AND VALIANT, A GRACIOUS PERSON.
BUT YET I CANNOT LOVE HIM.
HE MIGHT HAVE TOOK HIS ANSWER LONG AGO.
IF I DID LOVE YOU IN MY MASTER'S FLAME WITH SUCH A SUFFERING, IN YOUR DENIAL I WOULD FIND NO SENSE.
I WOULD NOT UNDERSTAND IT.
WHY, WHAT WOULD YOU DO?
MAKE ME A WILLOW CABIN AT YOUR GATE...
AND CALL UPON MY SOUL WITHIN THE HOUSE.

GET YOU TO YOUR LORD. LET HIM SEND NO MORE...
UNLESS, PERCHANCE, *YOU* COME TO ME AGAIN, TO TELL ME HOW HE TAKES IT.
I THANK YOU FOR YOUR PAINS.
LADY, KEEP YOUR PURSE.
MY MASTER, NOT MYSELF, LACKS RECOMPENSE.
FAREWELL, FAIR CRUELTY.

NOT TOO FAST!
HOW NOW?
EVEN SO QUICKLY MAY ONE CATCH THE PLAGUE?
METHINKS I FEEL THIS YOUTH'S PERFECTIONS WITH AN INVISIBLE AND SUBTLE STEALTH, TO CREEP IN AT MINE EYES.
WELL, LET IT BE.
WHAT, HO, MALVOLIO!

HE LEFT THIS RING BEHIND HIM.
RUN AFTER THAT MESSENGER.
TELL HIM I'LL NONE OF IT.
DESIRE HIM NOT TO FLATTER HIS LORD, NOR HOLD HIM UP WITH HOPES.
IF THAT THE YOUTH WILL COME THIS WAY TOMORROW, I'LL GIVE HIM REASONS FOR IT.
HIE THEE, MALVOLIO.
MADAM, I WILL.

I DO I KNOW NOT WHAT, AND FEAR TO FIND MINE EYE TOO GREAT A FLATTERER FOR MY MIND.
FATE, SHOW THY FORCE. OURSELVES WE DO NOT OWE.
WHAT IS DECREED MUST BE, AND BE THIS SO!

WILL YOU NOT THAT I GO WITH YOU?
MY FATHER WAS SEBASTIAN OF MESSALINE WHOM YOU HAVE HEARD OF.
HE LEFT BEHIND HIM MYSELF AND A SISTER, BOTH BORN IN AN HOUR.

BY YOUR PATIENCE, NO.
THE MALIGNANCY OF MY FATE MIGHT DISTEMPER YOURS.
I CRAVE YOUR LEAVE THAT I MAY BEAR MY EVILS ALONE.
MY NAME IS SEBASTIAN.
IF THE HEAVENS HAD BEEN PLEASED, WOULD WE HAD SO ENDED! BUT YOU, SIR, TOOK ME FROM THE SEA.
MY SISTER DROWNED.
ALAS THE DAY!

A LADY, IT WAS SAID, MUCH RESEMBLED ME.
SHE IS DROWNED WITH SALT WATER, THOUGH I DROWN HER REMEMBRANCE AGAIN WITH MORE.
LET ME BE YOUR SERVANT.
IF YOU WILL NOT UNDO WHAT YOU HAVE DONE — THAT IS, KILL HIM WHOM YOU HAVE RECOVERED — DESIRE IT NOT.

I AM BOUND TO COUNT ORSINO'S COURT.
FAREWELL.
THE GODS GO WITH THEE!
I HAVE MANY ENEMIES IN ORSINO'S COURT, ELSE WOULD I VERY SHORTLY SEE THEE THERE.
BUT COME WHAT MAY,
DANGER SHALL SEEM SPORT...
AND I WILL GO.
CLENCH

THE COUNTESS OLIVIA RETURNS THIS RING TO YOU, SIR.
SHE ADDS THAT YOU SHOULD PUT YOUR LORD INTO ASSURANCE SHE WILL NONE OF HIM.
SHE TOOK THE RING OF ME.
I'LL NONE OF IT.
HER WILL IS IT SHOULD BE RETURNED.
IF IT BE WORTH STOOPING FOR, THERE IT LIES.
IF NOT, BE IT HIS THAT FINDS IT.
?

I LEFT NO RING WITH HER. WHAT MEANS THIS LADY?
DUNK
SHE LOVES ME, SURE.
NONE OF MY LORD'S RING?
WHY, HE SENT HER NONE.
TRMP
TRMP
TRMP
I AM THE MAN!
IF IT BE SO, POOR LADY, SHE WERE BETTER LOVE A DREAM!
TRMP
TRMP
TRMP

DISGUISE, I SEE THOU ART A WICKEDNESS.
MY MASTER LOVES HER DEARLY...
AND I, POOR MONSTER, FOND AS MUCH ON HIM...

AND SHE, MISTAKEN, SEEMS TO DOTE ON ME.
WHAT WILL BECOME OF THIS?
1+1+1=2?
O TIME, THOU MUST UNTANGLE THIS, NOT I!
IT IS TOO HARD A KNOT FOR ME TO UNTIE.

DO NOT OUR LIVES CONSIST OF THE FOUR ELEMENTS?
I THINK IT RATHER CONSISTS OF EATING AND DRINKING.
HOO
HOO
THOU ART A SCHOLAR.
LET US THEREFORE EAT AND DRINK.
MARIA, I SAY! A STOUP OF WINE.
CLICK

!
WELCOME, ASS.
THE FOOL HAS AN EXCELLENT BREATH TO SING.
NOD NOD
WOULD YOU HAVE A LOVE SONG?
ROLL
WHAT IS LOVE? 'TIS NOT HEREAFTER, PRESENT MIRTH HATH PRESENT LAUGHTER, WHAT'S TO COME IS STILL UNSURE.
IN DELAY THERE LIES NO PLENTY. THEN COME KISS ME, SWEET AND TWENTY. YOUTH'S A STUFF WILL NOT ENDURE.
CLUNK

WHAT A CATERWAULING DO YOU KEEP HERE!
MY LADY CALLED UP MALVOLIO AND BID HIM TURN YOU OUT OF DOORS.
MALVOLIO'S A PEG-A-RAMSEY, AND –
THREE MERRY MEN BE WE!
AM NOT I CONSANGUINEOUS? AM I NOT OF HER BLOOD?
!
O, THE TWELFTH DAY OF DECEMBER –

FOR THE LOVE O' GOD, PEACE!
MY MASTERS, ARE YOU MAD?
DO YE MAKE AN ALE-HOUSE OF MY LADY'S HOUSE?
IS THERE NO RESPECT OF PLACE, PERSONS NOR TIME IN YOU?
SCOLDED
BURP

SIR TOBY, MY LADY BADE ME TELL YOU THAT, IF YOU CAN SEPARATE YOURSELF AND YOUR MISDEMEANOURS, YOU ARE WELCOME TO THE HOUSE.
IF NOT, SHE IS VERY WILLING TO BID YOU FAREWELL.
FAREWELL, DEAR HEART, SINCE I MUST NEEDS BE GONE.
GUH
NAY, GOOD SIR TOBY.
HIS EYES DO SHOW HIS DAYS ARE ALMOST DONE.
SNIFF
ART ANY MORE THAN A STEWARD?
DOST THOU THINK, BECAUSE THOU ART VIRTUOUS, THERE SHALL BE NO MORE CAKES AND ALE?
AND GINGER SHALL BE HOT IN THE MOUTH TOO.

A STOUP OF WINE, MARIA!
BANG

MISTRESS MARY, IF YOU PRIZED MY LADY'S FAVOUR, YOU WOULD NOT GIVE MEANS FOR THIS UNCIVIL RULE.

SWISH
SHE SHALL KNOW OF IT.

HMPF

SLAM

SWEET SIR TOBY, BE PATIENT FOR TONIGHT.
SINCE THE YOUTH OF THE COUNT'S WAS TODAY WITH MY LADY, SHE IS MUCH OUT OF QUIET.
PAT
PAT
FOR MONSIEUR MALVOLIO...
LET ME ALONE WITH HIM.
TELL US SOMETHING OF HIM.
HE IS A KIND OF PURITAN.
O, IF I THOUGHT THAT, I'D BEAT HIM LIKE A DOG.

THE DEVIL PURITAN SO CRAMMED, AS HE THINKS, WITH EXCELLENCIES, THAT IT IS HIS FAITH THAT ALL THAT LOOK ON HIM LOVE HIM.
BLING
ON THAT VICE IN HIM WILL MY REVENGE FIND NOTABLE CAUSE TO WORK.
WHAT WILT THOU DO?

I WILL DROP IN HIS WAY SOME EPISTLES OF LOVE, WHEREIN HE SHALL FIND HIMSELF MOST FEELINGLY PERSONATED.
I CAN WRITE VERY LIKE MY LADY.
WE CAN HARDLY MAKE DISTINCTION OF OUR HANDS.
EXCELLENT! I SMELL A DEVICE.
HE SHALL THINK, BY THE LETTERS THAT THOU WILT DROP, THAT MY NIECE IS IN LOVE WITH HIM.
PURRR
MY PURPOSE IS INDEED A HORSE OF THAT COLOUR.
SMACK

HI HI
AND YOUR HORSE NOW WOULD MAKE HIM AN ASS.
O, 'TWILL BE ADMIRABLE!
CLAP CLAP
SPORT ROYAL, I WARRANT YOU.
?
I WILL PLANT YOU TWO — AND LET THE FOOL MAKE A THIRD — WHERE HE SHALL FIND THE LETTER.
OBSERVE HIS CONSTRUCTION OF IT.
FOR THIS NIGHT, TO BED, AND DREAM ON THE EVENT.

WHOOOOOOO
GIVE ME SOME MUSIC.
THAT ANTIQUE SONG WE HEARD LAST NIGHT
METHOUGHT DID RELIEVE MY PASSION MUCH.
HE IS NOT HERE, YOUR LORDSHIP, THAT SHOULD SING IT.
WHOOOO
WHO WAS IT?
FESTE, THE JESTER THAT THE LADY OLIVIA'S FATHER TOOK MUCH DELIGHT IN.
SEEK HIM OUT AND PLAY THE TUNE THE WHILE.

COME HITHER, BOY.
IF EVER THOU SHALT LOVE, REMEMBER ME.
FOR SUCH AS I AM, ALL TRUE LOVERS ARE.
HOW DOST THOU LIKE THIS TUNE?
IT GIVES ECHO TO WHERE LOVE IS THRONED.

THOU DOST SPEAK MASTERLY.

THINE EYE HATH STAYED UPON SOME FAVOUR THAT IT LOVES, HATH IT NOT, BOY?

A LITTLE, BY YOUR FAVOUR.

TOO OLD, BY HEAVEN!
LET THE WOMAN TAKE AN ELDER THAN HERSELF, SO WEARS SHE TO HIM.
FOR WOMEN ARE AS ROSES WHOSE FAIR FLOWER, BEING ONCE DISPLAYED, DOTH FALL THAT VERY HOUR.
AND SO THEY ARE, ALAS – TO DIE, EVEN WHEN THEY TO PERFECTION GROW!
O, FELLOW, COME,
THE SONG WE HAD LAST NIGHT.
ARE YOU READY, SIR?

COME AWAY, COME AWAY, DEATH, AND IN SAD CYPRESS LET ME BE LAID.
FLY AWAY, FLY AWAY, BREATH, I AM SLAIN BY A FAIR CRUEL MAID.
MY SHROUD OF WHITE, STUCK ALL WITH YEW, O PREPARE IT!
MY PART OF DEATH NO ONE SO TRUE DID SHARE IT.

THERE'S FOR THY PAINS.
NO PAINS, SIR. I TAKE PLEASURE IN SINGING.
I'LL PAY THY PLEASURE, THEN.
TRULY, SIR, AND PLEASURE WILL BE PAID, ONE TIME OR ANOTHER.
NOW THE MELANCHOLY GOD PROTECT THEE!
FAREWELL.

ONCE MORE, CESARIO, GET THEE TO YOND SOVEREIGN CRUELTY.
TELL HER MY LOVE PRIZES NOT QUANTITY OF LANDS THAT FORTUNE HATH BESTOWED UPON HER.
TELL HER 'TIS THAT MIRACLE THAT NATURE PRANKS HER IN ATTRACTS MY SOUL.
WHOOOOOO
BUT IF SHE CANNOT LOVE YOU, SIR?
I CANNOT BE SO ANSWERED.

SAY THAT SOME LADY HATH AS GREAT A PANG OF HEART AS YOU HAVE FOR OLIVIA.
YOU CANNOT LOVE HER. YOU TELL HER SO.
MUST SHE NOT THEN BE ANSWERED?
THERE IS NO WOMAN CAN BIDE THE BEATING OF SO STRONG A PASSION AS LOVE DOTH GIVE MY HEART.
MAKE NO COMPARE BETWEEN THAT LOVE A WOMAN CAN BEAR ME AND THAT I OWE OLIVIA.
AY, BUT I KNOW –
WHAT DOST THOU KNOW?

TOO WELL WHAT LOVE WOMEN TO MEN MAY OWE.
MY FATHER HAD A DAUGHTER LOVED A MAN,
AS IT MIGHT BE PERHAPS, WERE I A WOMAN, I SHOULD YOUR LORDSHIP.
AND WHAT'S HER HISTORY?

A BLANK, MY LORD.
SHE NEVER TOLD HER LOVE, BUT LET CONCEALMENT, LIKE A WORM IN THE BUD, FEED ON HER DAMASK CHEEK.
SHE PINED IN THOUGHT, AND WITH A GREEN AND YELLOW MELANCHOLY, SAT SMILING AT GRIEF.
WAS NOT THIS LOVE, INDEED?

BUT DIED
THY SISTER
OF HER LOVE,
MY BOY?
I AM ALL
THE DAUGHTERS
OF MY FATHER'S
HOUSE, AND ALL
THE BROTHERS
TOO...
AND YET
I KNOW
NOT.

SIGH
SIR, SHALL I
TO THIS LADY?
AY, TO HER
IN HASTE.

SAY MY
LOVE CAN
BIDE NO
DENY.

SIGNIOR FABIAN!

WOULDST THOU NOT BE GLAD TO HAVE THE RASCALLY SHEEP-BITER COME BY SOME NOTABLE SHAME?

I WOULD EXULT, MAN.

HE BROUGHT ME OUT OF FAVOUR WITH MY LADY ABOUT A BEAR-BAITING HERE.

OOFF

WE WILL FOOL HIM BLACK AND BLUE –

SHALL WE NOT, SIR ANDREW?

HERE COMES THE LITTLE VILLAIN.
GET YE ALL THREE INTO THE BOX-TREE.
MALVOLIO'S COMING DOWN THIS WALK.
FLAP
FLAP
OBSERVE HIM,
FOR I KNOW THIS LETTER WILL MAKE A CONTEMPLATIVE IDIOT OF HIM.
HERE COMES THE TROUT THAT MUST BE CAUGHT WITH TICKLING.

FORTUNE, ALL IS FORTUNE.
MARIA ONCE TOLD ME SHE DID AFFECT ME...
AND I HAVE HEARD HERSELF COME THUS NEAR, THAT SHOULD SHE FANCY, IT SHOULD BE ONE OF MY COMPLEXION.
HERE'S AN OVERWEENING ROGUE!
O, PEACE!
CONTEMPLATION MAKES A RARE TURKEY-COCK OF HIM.

TO BE COUNT MALVOLIO –
HAVING BEEN THREE MONTHS MARRIED TO HER, SITTING IN MY VELVET GOWN,
HAVING COME FROM A DAY-BED WHERE I HAVE LEFT OLIVIA...
NOW HE'S DEEPLY IN! LOOK HOW IMAGINATION BLOWS HIM.
SLEEPING.
FIRE AND BRIMSTONE!

AND THEN TO ASK FOR MY KINSMAN TOBY.
BOLTS AND SHACKLES!
?
...
O, PEACE!
MMF!
I FROWN THE WHILE, AND PERCHANCE WIND UP MY WATCH, OR PLAY WITH SOME RICH JEWEL.
TOBY APPROACHES,
CURTSIES THERE TO ME.
SHALL THIS FELLOW LIVE?

I EXTEND MY HAND TO HIM THUS, SAYING, "COUSIN TOBY, MY FORTUNES HAVING CAST ME ON YOUR NIECE, GIVE ME THIS PREROGATIVE OF SPEECH...
WHAT, WHAT?
"YOU MUST AMEND YOUR DRUNKENNESS...
OUT, SCAB!
NAY, PATIENCE, OR WE BREAK THE SINEWS OF OUR PLOT.
"BESIDES, YOU WASTE THE TREASURE OF YOUR TIME WITH A FOOLISH KNIGHT."
THAT'S ME, I WARRANT YOU.

WHAT HAVE WE HERE?

BY MY LIFE, THIS IS MY LADY'S HAND.
THESE BE HER VERY C'S, HER U'S AND HER T'S...
AND THUS MAKES SHE HER GREAT P'S...

TO WHOM SHOULD THIS BE?

"TO THE UNKNOWN BELOVED..."
'TIS MY LADY.

...

CRACK
"JOVE KNOWS I LOVE,
BUT WHO?"
"LIPS, DO NOT MOVE,
NO MAN MUST KNOW."
IF THIS SHOULD BE THEE, MALVOLIO?
HANG THEE, BROCK!
SWISH
"I MAY COMMAND WHERE I ADORE..."
"M, O, A, I, DOTH SWAY MY LIFE."

A RIDDLE!
EXCELLENT WENCH, SAY I.
"M, O, A, I, DOTH SWAY MY LIFE."
LET ME SEE, LET ME SEE...

WHAT DISH OF POISON HAS SHE DRESSED HIM!
"I MAY COMMAND WHERE I ADORE..."

FLAP
FLAP
WHY, SHE MAY COMMAND ME!
I SERVE HER,
SHE IS MY LADY.

WHAT SHOULD THAT ALPHABETICAL POSITION PORTEND?
"M, O, A, I."
M
O
"M" —
MALVOLIO!
WHY, THAT BEGINS MY NAME.

MALVOLIO
"M, O, A, I."
EVERY ONE OF THESE LETTERS ARE IN MY NAME.
"M"!
BUT THEN THERE IS NO CONSONANCY IN THE SEQUEL.
"A" SHOULD FOLLOW, BUT "O" DOES.
I'LL CUDGEL HIM AND MAKE HIM CRY "O!"
SOFT! HERE FOLLOWS PROSE.

"I AM ABOVE THEE, BUT BE NOT AFRAID OF GREATNESS."
"SOME ARE BORN GREAT..."
"SOME ACHIEVE GREATNESS..."

"AND SOME HAVE GREATNESS THRUST UPON THEM."
"CAST THY HUMBLE SLOUGH AND APPEAR FRESH."
"BE OPPOSITE WITH A KINSMAN,
SURLY WITH SERVANTS."
"PUT THYSELF INTO THE TRICK OF SINGULARITY."
BURP
"SHE THUS ADVISES THEE THAT SIGHS FOR THEE."

"REMEMBER WHO COMMENDED THY YELLOW STOCKINGS..."
"AND WISHED TO SEE THEE EVER CROSS-GARTERED."
"GO TO, THOU ART MADE, IF THOU DESIREST TO BE SO."
"IF NOT, LET ME SEE THEE A STEWARD STILL,
THE FELLOW OF SERVANTS, AND NOT WORTHY TO TOUCH FORTUNE'S FINGERS."
"FAREWELL. THE FORTUNATE UNHAPPY."
Farewell
The Fortunate Unhappy

EVERY REASON EXCITES TO THIS, THAT MY LADY LOVES ME.
SHE DID COMMEND MY YELLOW STOCKINGS OF LATE.
SHE DID PRAISE MY LEG BEING CROSS-GARTERED.
AND IN THIS SHE MANIFESTS HERSELF TO MY LOVE.
I AM HAPPY.
JOVE AND MY STARS BE PRAISED!

HERE IS YET A POSTSCRIPT.
"IF THOU ENTERTAINEST MY LOVE, LET IT APPEAR IN THY SMILING..."
"THY SMILES BECOME THEE WELL."
"THEREFORE IN MY PRESENCE SMILE, DEAR MY SWEET."
I WILL SMILE.
I WILL DO EVERYTHING THAT THOU WILT HAVE ME.
BOING
BOING
BOING

HAHA HA HA
HAHA
HERE COMES MY NOBLE GULL-CATCHER.
WHY, THOU HAST PUT HIM IN SUCH A DREAM, THAT WHEN THE IMAGE OF IT LEAVES HIM, HE MUST RUN MAD.
SAY TRUE. DOES IT WORK UPON HIM?
LIKE AQUA-VITAE WITH A MIDWIFE.

HE WILL COME TO HER IN YELLOW STOCKINGS –
A COLOUR SHE ABHORS.
TAK
CROSS-GARTERED –
A FASHION SHE DETESTS.

HE WILL SMILE UPON HER — WHICH WILL BE SO UNSUITABLE TO HER DISPOSITION,
BEING ADDICTED TO MELANCHOLY AS SHE IS...
IT CANNOT BUT TURN HIM INTO A NOTABLE CONTEMPT.
THOU MOST EXCELLENT DEVIL OF WIT!
DOFF

SQUEAK
SQUEAK
SQUEAK
SQUEAK
SQUEAK
SQUEAK
ART NOT THOU THE LADY OLIVIA'S FOOL?
NO INDEED, SIR, THE LADY OLIVIA HAS NO FOOL TILL SHE BE MARRIED.
SQUEAK
SQUEAK
SQUEAK
SQUEAK
I SAW THEE AT THE COUNT ORSINO'S.
FOOLERY, SIR, DOES WALK ABOUT LIKE THE SUN —
IT SHINES EVERYWHERE.
SQUEAK
I'LL NO MORE WITH THEE.
PATA
PATA
THERE'S EXPENSES FOR THEE.

NOW JOVE SEND THEE A BEARD!
SWOOSH
I'LL TELL THEE, I AM ALMOST SICK FOR ONE...
THOUGH I WOULD NOT HAVE IT GROW ON MY CHIN.
YES...
WOULD NOT A PAIR OF THESE HAVE BRED, SIR?
YES, BEING KEPT TOGETHER AND PUT TO USE.

WHO YOU ARE AND WHAT YOU WOULD ARE OUT OF MY WELKIN.
I MIGHT SAY "ELEMENT"...
BUT THE WORD IS OVERWORN.
BEAM
THIS FELLOW IS WISE ENOUGH TO PLAY THE FOOL.
HE MUST OBSERVE THEIR MOOD ON WHOM HE JESTS.
TAK
TAK
HUFF
HUFF
THIS IS A PRACTICE AS FULL OF LABOUR AS A WISE MAN'S ART.

TAK
TAK TAK
MOST EXCELLENT ACCOMPLISHED LADY,
THE HEAVENS RAIN ODOURS ON YOU!
HUFF
HUFF
LET THE GARDEN DOOR BE SHUT, AND LEAVE ME TO MY HEARING.
SIGH

GIVE ME YOUR HAND, SIR.

MY DUTY, MADAM, AND MOST HUMBLE SERVICE.

I THINK NOT ON HIM.
FOR HIS THOUGHTS, WOULD THEY WERE BLANKS, RATHER THAN FILLED WITH ME!
MADAM, I COME TO WHET YOUR GENTLE THOUGHTS ON HIS BEHALF –
I BADE YOU NEVER SPEAK AGAIN OF HIM.
BUT, WOULD YOU UNDERTAKE ANOTHER SUIT,
I HAD RATHER HEAR YOU TO SOLICIT THAT.
DEAR LADY –
I DID SEND A RING IN CHASE OF YOU.
SO DID I ABUSE MYSELF, MY SERVANT, AND, I FEAR ME, YOU.

TO FORCE THAT ON YOU, IN SHAMEFUL CUNNING, WHICH YOU KNEW NONE OF YOURS...
WHAT MIGHT YOU THINK?
LET ME HEAR YOU SPEAK.
I PITY YOU.
THAT'S A DEGREE TO LOVE.
NO, FOR 'TIS A VULGAR PROC THAT VERY OF WE PITY ENEMIES.

ENEMY
O WORLD, HOW APT THE POOR ARE TO BE PROUD!
BE NOT AFRAID, GOOD YOUTH,
I WILL NOT HAVE YOU.
AND YET, WHEN YOUTH IS COME TO HARVEST...
YOUR WIFE IS LIKE TO REAP A PROPER MAN.

THERE LIES YOUR WAY,
DUE-WEST.
THEN WESTWARD-HO!
SLAM
STAY.
TELL ME WHAT THOU THINK'ST OF ME.
THAT YOU DO THINK YOU ARE NOT WHAT YOU ARE.
I THINK THE SAME OF YOU.

THEN THINK YOU RIGHT.
I AM NOT WHAT I AM.
CESARIO, BY THE ROSES OF THE SPRING...
BY MAIDHOOD, HONOUR, TRUTH AND EVERYTHING...
I LOVE THEE SO THAT MAUGRE ALL THY PRIDE, NOR WIT NOR REASON CAN MY PASSION HIDE.

DO NOT EXTORT THY REASONS FROM THIS CLAUSE.
BUT RATHER REASON THUS:
LOVE SOUGHT IS GOOD...
BUT GIVEN UNSOUGHT IS BETTER.
BY INNOCENCE I SWEAR, AND BY MY YOUTH,
I HAVE ONE HEART, ONE BOSOM, AND ONE TRUTH.

AND THAT NO WOMAN HAS...
NOR NEVER NONE SHALL MISTRESS BE OF IT...
DRAG
DRAG
SHIKA
SHAKA
SAVE I ALONE.
AND SO ADIEU, GOOD MADAM. NEVER MORE
WILL I MY MASTER'S TEARS TO YOU DEPLORE.
YET COME AGAIN!
FOR THOU PERHAPS MAYST MOVE THAT HEART, WHICH NOW ABHORS, TO LIKE HIS LOVE.

NO, I'LL NOT STAY A JOT LONGER.
THY REASON,
GIVE THY REASON.
I SAW YOUR NIECE DO MORE FAVOURS TO THE COUNT'S SERVINGMAN THAN EVER SHE BESTOWED UPON ME.
WILL YOU MAKE AN ASS OF ME?
SHE DID SHOW FAVOUR TO THE YOUTH ONLY TO EXASPERATE YOU.

YOU SHOULD THEN HAVE ACCOSTED HER,
AND WITH SOME EXCELLENT JESTS BANGED THE YOUTH INTO DUMBNESS.
YOU ARE NOW SAILED INTO THE NORTH OF MY LADY'S OPINION,
WHERE YOU WILL HANG LIKE AN ICICLE ON A DUTCHMAN'S BEARD...
UNLESS YOU REDEEM IT BY SOME VALOUR.

HURT HIM IN ELEVEN PLACES.
MY NIECE SHALL TAKE NOTE OF IT.
CHALLENGE THE COUNT'S YOUTH TO FIGHT.
THERE IS NO LOVE-BROKER CAN MORE PREVAIL WITH WOMAN THAN REPORT OF VALOUR.
THERE IS NO WAY BUT THIS, SIR ANDREW.

THUNK
WILL EITHER OF YOU BEAR ME A CHALLENGE TO HIM?
SMACK
GO,
WRITE IT IN A MARTIAL HAND.
LET THERE BE GALL ENOUGH IN THY INK.
CLCK
THOUGH THOU WRITE WITH A GOOSE-PEN, NO MATTER.
ABOUT IT!
NOD
NOD

WE SHALL HAVE A RARE LETTER FROM HIM.
BY ALL MEANS STIR ON THE YOUTH TO AN ANSWER.
I THINK OXEN AND WAIN-ROPES CANNOT HALE THEM TOGETHER.
IF YOU WILL LAUGH YOURSELVES INTO STITCHES, FOLLOW ME.
YOND GULL MALVOLIO IS IN YELLOW STOCKINGS!

AND CROSS-GARTERED?
MOST VILLAINOUSLY.
HE DOES OBEY EVERY POINT OF THE LETTER THAT I DROPPED TO BETRAY HIM.
I KNOW MY LADY WILL STRIKE HIM.
IF SHE DO, HE'LL SMILE AND TAKE IT FOR A GREAT FAVOUR.
COME, BRING US WHERE HE IS.

MY KIND ANTONIO, WHAT'S TO DO?
SHALL WE GO SEE THIS TOWN?
TOMORROW, SIR.
BEST, FIRST, GO SEE YOUR LODGING.
I AM NOT WEARY.
LET US SATISFY OUR EYES WITH THE THINGS OF FAME THAT DO RENOWN THIS CITY.
WOULD YOU'D PARDON ME.
I DO NOT WITHOUT DANGER WALK THESE STREETS.

ONCE IN A SEA-FIGHT 'GAINST THE COUNT...
I DID SOME SERVICE.
BELIKE YOU SLEW GREAT NUMBER OF HIS PEOPLE?
KABOOM
THE OFFENCE IS NOT OF SUCH A BLOODY NATURE...
ALBEIT, IF I BE LAPSED IN THIS PLACE, I SHALL PAY DEAR.

DO NOT THEN WALK TOO OPEN.
!
FSH
IT DOTH NOT FIT ME.
TUG
HOLD, SIR...
IN THE SOUTH SUBURBS, AT THE ELEPHANT, IS BEST TO LODGE.
HERE'S MY PURSE.
WHILES YOU BEGUILE THE TIME WITH VIEWING OF THE TOWN, THERE SHALL YOU HAVE ME.

WHY YOUR PURSE?
YOUR STORE, I THINK, IS NOT FOR IDLE MARKETS, SIR.
I'LL BE YOUR PURSE-BEARER AND LEAVE YOU FOR AN HOUR.
TO THE ELEPHANT.
I DO REMEMBER.

SIGH

WHERE'S MALVOLIO?

HE IS SAD AND CIVIL, AND SUITS WELL WITH MY FORTUNES.

HE'S COMING, MADAM.

BUT IN VERY STRANGE MANNER.

HE IS SURE POSSESSED.

I AM AS MAD AS HE...
IF SAD AND MERRY MADNESS EQUAL BE.
SWEET LADY,
HO,
HO!
KLACK

SMILEST THOU?
SAD, LADY?
I COULD BE SAD.
THIS DOES MAKE SOME OBSTRUCTION IN THE BLOOD, THIS CROSS-GARTERING.
BUT WHAT OF THAT?
I SENT FOR THEE UPON A SAD OCCASION.
WHAT IS THE MATTER WITH THEE?
NOT BLACK IN MY MIND, THOUGH YELLOW IN MY LEGS.
IT DID COME TO HIS HANDS,
AND COMMANDS SHALL BE EXECUTED.

TO BED?
WILT THOU GO TO BED, MALVOLIO?
"AY, SWEETHEART!
AND I'LL COME TO THEE."
GOD COMFORT THEE!
"BE NOT AFRAID OF GREATNESS."
'TWAS WELL WRIT.
WHAT MEANEST THOU BY THAT, MALVOLIO?
"REMEMBER WHO COMMENDED THY YELLOW STOCKINGS..."
WHY, THIS IS MIDSUMMER MADNESS!

MADAM, THE YOUNG GENTLEMAN OF THE COUNT ORSINO'S IS RETURNED.
I'LL COME TO HIM.
MARIA, LET THIS FELLOW BE LOOKED TO.
WHERE'S MY COUSIN TOBY?
LET SOME OF MY PEOPLE HAVE A SPECIAL CARE OF HIM.

NO WORSE MAN THAN SIR TOBY TO LOOK TO ME?
THIS CONCURS DIRECTLY WITH THE LETTER...
"LET THIS FELLOW BE LOOKED TO"!
"FELLOW"!
NOT "MALVOLIO".
NOTHING CAN COME BETWEEN ME AND THE FULL PROSPECT OF MY HOPES.

IF ALL THE DEVILS OF HELL POSSESSED HIM, YET I'LL SPEAK TO HIM.
GO OFF, I DISCARD YOU.
LET ME ENJOY MY PRIVATE.
LO, HOW THE FIEND SPEAKS WITHIN HIM!
MALVOLIO, DEFY THE DEVIL!
HE'S AN ENEMY TO MANKIND.

DO YOU KNOW WHAT YOU SAY?
GENTLY, GENTLY. THE FIEND IS ROUGH, AND WILL NOT BE ROUGHLY USED.
GET HIM TO SAY HIS PRAYERS, GOOD SIR TOBY.
MY PRAYERS, MINX?
SHOVE
NO, I WARRANT YOU, HE WILL NOT HEAR OF GODLINESS.

GO, HANG YOURSELVES ALL!
YOU ARE IDLE SHALLOW THINGS.
I AM NOT OF YOUR ELEMENT.
IS IT POSSIBLE?
IF THIS WERE PLAYED UPON A STAGE, I COULD CONDEMN IT AS AN IMPROBABLE FICTION.

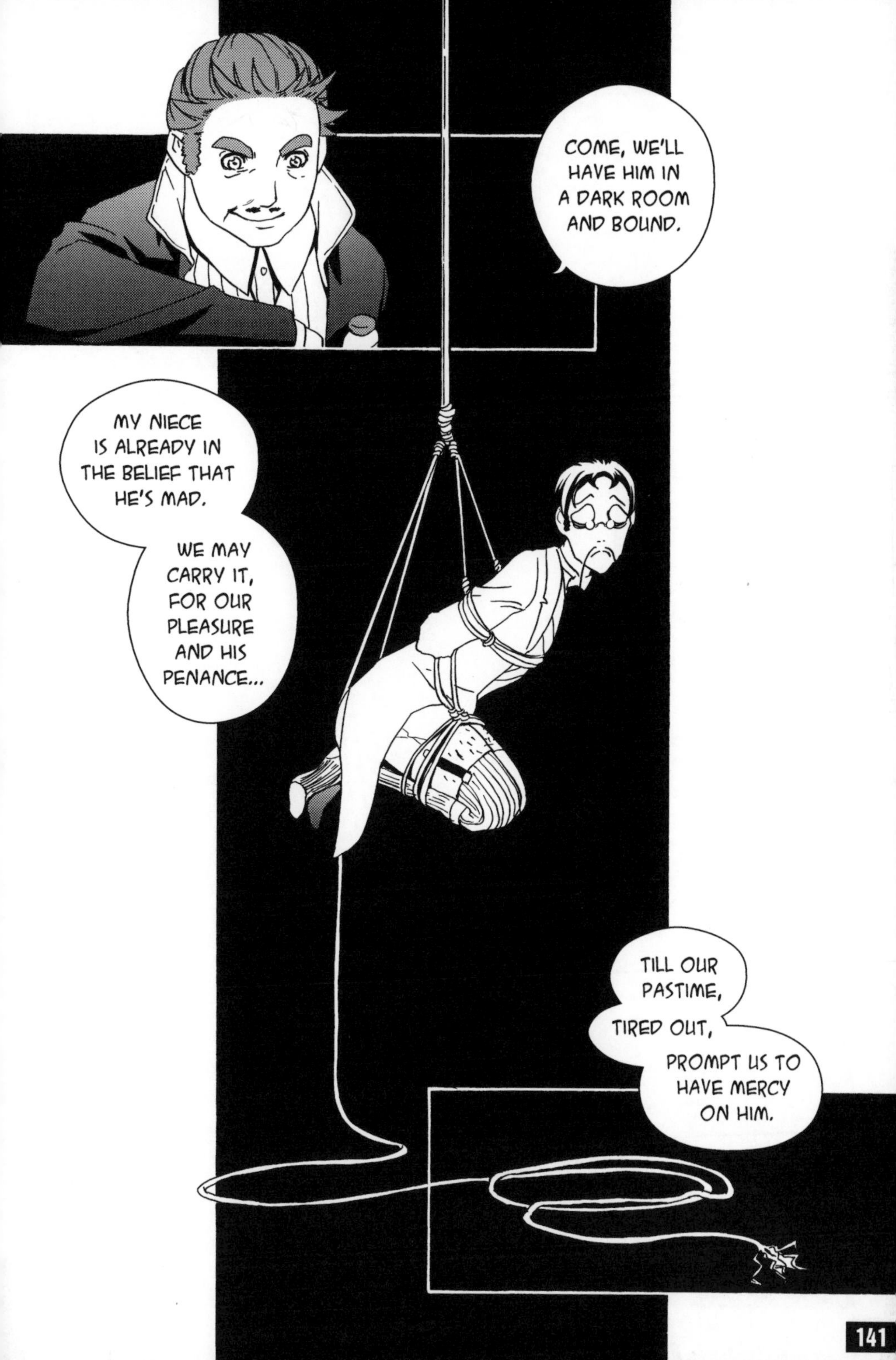
COME, WE'LL HAVE HIM IN A DARK ROOM AND BOUND.
MY NIECE IS ALREADY IN THE BELIEF THAT HE'S MAD.
WE MAY CARRY IT, FOR OUR PLEASURE AND HIS PENANCE...
TILL OUR PASTIME,
TIRED OUT,
PROMPT US TO HAVE MERCY ON HIM.

HERE'S THE CHALLENGE.
I WARRANT THERE'S VINEGAR AND PEPPER IN IT.

"YOUTH, WHATSOEVER THOU ART, THOU ART BUT A SCURVY FELLOW."

"IF IT BE THY CHANCE TO KILL ME,
THOU KILL'ST ME LIKE A ROGUE AND VILLAIN."
"THY SWORN ENEMY, ANDREW AGUECHEEK."

...
...

GO, SIR ANDREW. SCOUT FOR HIM AT THE CORNER OF THE ORCHARD.
AWAY.
NOW WILL NOT I DELIVER HIS LETTER.
THIS WILL BREED NO TERROR IN THE YOUTH.
HE WILL FIND IT COMES FROM A CLODPOLL.
HERE HE COMES WITH YOUR NIECE.
I WILL MEDITATE UPON SOME HORRID MESSAGE FOR A CHALLENGE.
RYTSCH

HERE, WEAR THIS JEWEL FOR ME. 'TIS MY PICTURE.
REFUSE IT NOT, IT HATH NO TONGUE TO VEX YOU.
WHAT SHALL YOU ASK OF ME THAT, HONOUR SAVED, MAY UPON ASKING GIVE?
YOUR TRUE LOVE FOR MY MASTER.
HOW WITH HONOUR MAY I GIVE HIM THAT WHICH I HAVE GIVEN TO YOU?
FARE THEE WELL.
A FIEND LIKE THEE MIGHT BEAR MY SOUL TO HELL.
DRIP

OF WHAT NATURE THE WRONGS ARE THOU HAST DONE HIM, I KNOW NOT.
BUT THY HUNTER ATTENDS THEE AT THE ORCHARD.
BE YARE IN THY PREPARATION, FOR THY ASSAILANT IS QUICK, SKILFUL AND DEADLY.
YOU MISTAKE, SIR.
I AM SURE NO MAN HATH ANY QUARREL TO ME.
YOU'LL FIND IT OTHERWISE, I ASSURE YOU.

I PRAY YOU, SIR, WHAT IS HE?
HE IS KNIGHT... BUT A DEVIL IN PRIVATE BRAWL.
SOULS AND BODIES HATH HE DIVORCED THREE.
I AM NO FIGHTER.
I HAVE HEARD OF SOME MEN THAT PUT QUARRELS PURPOSELY ON OTHERS TO TASTE THEIR VALOUR.
BELIKE THIS IS A MAN OF THAT QUIRK.
SIR, NO. HIS INDIGNATION DERIVES OUT OF A VERY COMPETENT INJURY.

THIS IS STRANGE.
I BESEECH YOU AS TO KNOW WHAT MY OFFENCE TO HIM IS.
I WILL DO SO.

MUNCH MUNCH
SIR, DO YOU KNOW OF THIS MATTER?

I KNOW THE KNIGHT IS INCENSED AGAINST YOU...
BUT NOTHING OF THE CIRCUMSTANCE.

WHY, MAN, HE'S A VERY DEVIL!
I HAVE NOT SEEN SUCH A FENCER!
I'LL NOT MEDDLE WITH HIM.
TUG
AY, BUT HE WILL NOT NOW BE PACIFIED.
LET HIM LET THE MATTER SLIP AND I'LL GIVE HIM MY HORSE!

THERE'S NO REMEDY, SIR.
HE WILL FIGHT WITH YOU FOR HIS OATH'S SAKE.
HE PROTESTS HE WILL NOT HURT YOU.
PRAY GOD DEFEND ME!
A LITTLE THING WOULD MAKE ME TELL THEM HOW MUCH I LACK OF A MAN.
COME, SIR ANDREW.
THE GENTLEMAN WILL, FOR HIS HONOUR'S SAKE, HAVE ONE BOUT WITH YOU.
BUT HE HAS PROMISED ME, AS HE IS A GENTLEMAN, HE WILL NOT HURT YOU.
PRAY GOD HE KEEP HIS OATH!
RATTLE
RATTLE
!

PUT UP
YOUR SWORD.
YOU, SIR?
WHY, WHAT ARE YOU?
IF THIS YOUNG GENTLEMAN HAVE DONE OFFENCE, I TAKE THE FAULT ON ME.
SWISH
ONE THAT FOR HIS LOVE DARES DO MORE THAN YOU HAVE HEARD HIM BRAG HE WILL.
NAY, IF YOU BE AN UNDERTAKER, I AM FOR YOU!
SIR TOBY, HOLD.
HERE COME THE OFFICERS.

PRAY, SIR, PUT YOUR SWORD UP, IF YOU PLEASE.
MARRY, WILL I, SIR.
AND FOR THAT I PROMISED YOU, I'LL BE AS GOOD AS MY WORD.
HE WILL BEAR YOU EASILY AND REINS WELL.
BUNK BUNK
THIS IS THE MAN.
ANTONIO, I ARREST THEE AT THE SUIT OF COUNT ORSINO.
YOU DO MISTAKE ME, SIR.

NO, SIR, I KNOW YOU WELL –
THOUGH YOU HAVE NO SEA-CAP ON YOUR HEAD.
THIS COMES WITH SEEKING YOU.

I MUST ENTREAT OF YOU SOME OF THAT MONEY.
NOW MY NECESSITY MAKES ME ASK YOU FOR MY PURSE.
YOU STAND AMAZED.
WHAT MONEY, SIR?
FOR THE FAIR KINDNESS YOU HAVE SHOWED ME, I'LL LEND YOU SOMETHING.
WILL YOU DENY ME NOW?
DO NOT TEMPT MY MISERY TO UPBRAID YOU WITH THOSE KINDNESSES THAT I HAVE DONE FOR YOU.
I KNOW OF NONE.
NOR KNOW I YOU BY VOICE OR ANY FEATURE.

O HEAVENS THEMSELVES!
COME, SIR.
LET ME SPEAK A LITTLE.
THIS YOUTH I SNATCHED OUT OF THE JAWS OF DEATH.
WHAT'S THAT TO US?
AWAY!
THOU HAST, SEBASTIAN, DONE GOOD FEATURE SHAME.
IN NATURE THERE'S NO BLEMISH BUT THE MIND.
NONE CAN BE CALLED DEFORMED BUT THE UNKIND.

PROVE TRUE, IMAGINATION...
O PROVE TRUE, THAT I, DEAR BROTHER, BE NOW TAKEN FOR YOU!
HE NAMED SEBASTIAN.
O, IF IT PROVE, TEMPESTS ARE KIND, AND SALT WAVES FRESH IN LOVE!
A VERY PALTRY BOY, LEAVING HIS FRIEND IN NECESSITY AND DENYING HIM!
I'LL AFTER HIM AGAIN AND BEAT HIM.

SQUEAK
SQUEAK
THOU ART A FOOLISH FELLOW.
LET ME BE CLEAR OF THEE.
SQUEAK
SQUEAK
NO, I DO NOT KNOW YOU.
NOR I AM NOT SENT TO YOU BY MY LADY.
NOR YOUR NAME IS NOT MASTER CESARIO.
SQUEAK
SQUEAK
SQUEAK
NOR THIS IS NOT MY NOSE NEITHER.
NOTHING THAT IS SO IS SO.
VENT THY FOLLY SOMEWHERE ELSE.
THOU KNOW'ST NOT ME.

"VENT" MY FOLLY?
UNGIRD THY STRANGENESS, AND TELL ME, WHAT I SHALL "VENT" TO MY LADY?
SHALL I "VENT" TO HER THAT THOU ART COMING?
THERE'S MONEY FOR THEE.
IF YOU TARRY LONGER I SHALL GIVE WORSE PAYMENT.
WISE MEN THAT GIVE FOOLS MONEY GET THEMSELVES A GOOD REPORT.
SQUEAK
SQUEAK

NOW, SIR, HAVE I MET YOU AGAIN?
TWACK!
THERE'S FOR YOU.
WHY, THERE'S FOR THEE!
ARE ALL THE PEOPLE MAD?
HOLD, SIR.

IF THOU DAR'ST TEMPT ME FURTHER, DRAW THY SWORD.
WHAT, WHAT?
THEN I MUST HAVE AN OUNCE OR TWO OF BLOOD FROM YOU.
HOLD, TOBY, ON THY LIFE.
UNGRACIOUS WRETCH.
OUT OF MY SIGHT!
BE NOT OFFENDED, DEAR CESARIO!

GO WITH ME TO MY HOUSE, AND HEAR HOW MANY FRUITLESS PRANKS THIS RUFFIAN HATH BOTCHED UP.
THOU SHALT NOT CHOOSE BUT GO. DO NOT DENY.
WOULD THOU BE RULED BY ME?
WHAT IS IN THIS?
I AM MAD, OR ELSE THIS IS A DREAM.
IF IT BE THUS TO DREAM, STILL LET ME SLEEP!

MADAM,
I WILL.

PUT ON THIS GOWN AND BEARD.
MAKE HIM BELIEVE THOU ART SIR TOPAS THE CURATE.
TO HIM, SIR TOPAS.
PEACE IN THIS PRISON!
WHO CALLS THERE?
SIR TOPAS THE CURATE, WHO COMES TO VISIT MALVOLIO THE LUNATIC.

SIR TOPAS, NEVER WAS MAN THUS WRONGED.
DO NOT THINK I AM MAD. THEY HAVE LAID ME HERE IN DARKNESS.
FIE, THOU DISHONEST SATAN!
SAY'ST THOU THE HOUSE IS DARK?
I AM NOT MAD, SIR TOPAS.
I SAY TO YOU THIS HOUSE IS DARK.

MADMAN, THOU ERREST.
I SAY THERE IS NO DARKNESS BUT IGNORANCE.
I SAY THERE WAS NEVER MAN THUS ABUSED!
I AM NO MORE MAD THAN YOU ARE!
FARE THEE WELL.
REMAIN THOU STILL IN DARKNESS.
THOU MIGHTST HAVE DONE THIS WITHOUT BEARD AND GOWN.
HE SEES THEE NOT.

BURP!
I WOULD WE WERE RID OF THIS KNAVERY.
FOR I AM NOW SO FAR IN OFFENCE WITH MY NIECE THAT I CANNOT PURSUE WITH ANY SAFETY THIS SPORT TO THE UPSHOT.
HEY, ROBIN, JOLLY ROBIN, TELL ME HOW THY LADY DOES.
FOOL!

DRIP
DROP
TREMBLE
THEY KEEP ME IN DARKNESS, SEND MINISTERS TO ME –
ASSES!
THEN YOU ARE MAD INDEED, IF YOU BE NO BETTER IN YOUR WITS THAN A FOOL.

GOOD FOOL, HELP ME TO A CANDLE, PEN, INK AND PAPER.
BANG
BANG
BANG
THE MINISTER IS HERE.
I WILL LIVE TO BE THANKFUL TO THEE FOR IT.
ALAS, SIR, HOW FELL YOU BESIDES YOUR FIVE WITS?
I AM AS WELL IN MY WITS, FOOL, AS THOU ART.
KNOCK
KNOCK

MALVOLIO, THY WITS THE HEAVENS RESTORE!
SIR TOPAS!
WHO, I, SIR? NOT I, SIR.
GOD BE WITH YOU, GOOD SIR TOPAS.
MARRY, AMEN.
FOOL, I SAY —
SOME INK, PAPER, AND LIGHT! AND CONVEY WHAT I WILL SET DOWN TO MY LADY.
IT SHALL ADVANTAGE THEE MORE THAN EVER THE BEARING OF LETTER DID.

I WILL HELP YOU TO IT.
BUT TELL ME TRUE, ARE YOU MAD OR DO YOU COUNTERFEIT?
BELIEVE ME, I AM NOT!
I'LL NEVER BELIEVE A MADMAN TILL I SEE HIS BRAINS.
I WILL FETCH YOU LIGHT, PAPER AND INK.
FOOL, I'LL REQUITE IT IN THE HIGHEST DEGREE.

WHERE'S ANTONIO, THEN?
I COULD NOT FIND HIM AT THE ELEPHANT.
HIS COUNSEL NOW MIGHT DO ME GOLDEN SERVICE.
I AM READY TO DISTRUST MINE EYES AND WRANGLE WITH MY REASON THAT PERSUADES ME THAT I AM MAD...
OR ELSE THE LADY'S MAD!

NOW GO WITH ME AND THIS HOLY MAN.
PLIGHT ME THE FULL ASSURANCE OF YOUR FAITH,
THAT MY JEALOUS AND DOUBTFUL SOUL MAY LIVE AT PEACE.
WHAT DO YOU SAY?
I'LL GO WITH YOU...
AND, HAVING SWORN TRUTH, EVER WILL BE TRUE.

VRMM
VRMMM
VRMMMM!!
SQUEAK
KLK

BELONG YOU TO THE LADY OLIVIA, FRIENDS?
AY, SIR, WE ARE SOME OF HER TRAPPINGS.
THERE'S GOLD. IF YOU WILL LET YOUR LADY KNOW I AM HERE TO SPEAK WITH HER...
AND BRING HER ALONG WITH YOU, IT MAY AWAKE MY BOUNTY FURTHER.
SIR, LULLABY YOUR BOUNTY TILL I COME AGAIN!

HERE COMES THE MAN THAT DID RESCUE ME.
THAT FACE I DO REMEMBER WELL...
YET WHEN I SAW IT LAST, IT WAS BESMEARED IN THE SMOKE OF WAR.
SHOVE
THIS IS ANTONIO THAT TOOK THE *PHOENIX* AND DID THE *TIGER* BOARD WHEN YOUR NEPHEW TITUS LOST HIS LEG.
KSH
HE DID ME KINDNESS, SIR...
BUT PUT STRANGE SPEECH UPON ME.

NOTABLE PIRATE!
THOU SALT-WATER THIEF!
WHAT FOOLISH BOLDNESS BROUGHT THEE TO THEIR MERCIES?
NOBLE SIR, I NEVER YET WAS THIEF OR PIRATE...
THOUGH, I CONFESS, ON GROUND ENOUGH,
ORSINO'S ENEMY.
THAT MOST INGRATEFUL BOY THERE BY YOUR SIDE FROM THE SEA DID I REDEEM.
HIS LIFE I GAVE HIM, AND DID THERETO ADD MY LOVE.

FOR HIS SAKE DID I EXPOSE MYSELF TO THE DANGER OF THIS ADVERSE TOWN.
HIS FALSE CUNNING DENIED ME MINE OWN PURSE, WHICH I HAD RECOMMENDED TO HIS USE NOT HALF AN HOUR BEFORE.
HOW CAN THIS BE?
WHEN CAME HE TO THIS TOWN?
TODAY, MY LORD.
AND FOR THREE MONTHS BEFORE, BOTH DAY AND NIGHT DID WE KEEP COMPANY.

THREE MONTHS THIS YOUTH HATH TENDED UPON ME.
FELLOW, THY WORDS ARE MADNESS.
TAKE HIM ASIDE.
CESARIO, YOU DO NOT KEEP PROMISE WITH ME.
TAK
TAK
TAK
MADAM?

GRACIOUS OLIVIA –
WHAT DO YOU SAY, CESARIO?
MY LORD WOULD SPEAK.
IF IT BE THE OLD TUNE, IT IS TO MINE EAR AS HOWLING AFTER MUSIC.

STILL SO CRUEL?
STILL SO CONSTANT, LORD.
YOU UNCIVIL LADY...
WHAT SHALL I DO?
EVEN WHAT IT PLEASE MY LORD THAT SHALL BECOME HIM.

I KNOW THE INSTRUMENT THAT SCREWS ME FROM MY TRUE PLACE IN YOUR FAVOUR.
BUT THIS YOUR MINION, WHOM I KNOW YOU LOVE...
HIM WILL I TEAR OUT OF THAT CRUEL EYE WHERE HE SITS CROWNED IN HIS MASTER'S SPITE.

COME, BOY, WITH ME.
MY THOUGHTS ARE RIPE IN MISCHIEF.
I'LL SACRIFICE THE LAMB THAT I DO LOVE TO SPITE A RAVEN'S HEART WITHIN A DOVE.
AND I, MOST WILLINGLY, TO DO YOU REST A THOUSAND DEATHS WOULD DIE.

WHERE GOES CESARIO?
AFTER HIM I LOVE MORE THAN I LOVE MY LIFE...
MORE THAN EVER I SHALL LOVE WIFE.
AH ME, HOW AM I BEGUILED!
WHO DOES BEGUILE YOU?
HAST THOU FORGOT THYSELF?
IS IT SO LONG?
CALL FORTH THE HOLY FATHER!

COME, AWAY!
CESARIO, HUSBAND, STAY.
"HUSBAND"?
AY, HUSBAND. CAN HE THAT DENY?

FATHER, I CHARGE THEE TO UNFOLD WHAT HATH PASSED BETWEEN THIS YOUTH AND ME.
A CONTRACT OF ETERNAL BOND OF LOVE.
CONFIRMED SINCE BUT TWO HOURS.
O, THOU DISSEMBLING CUB!
FAREWELL, AND TAKE HER.
BUT DIRECT THY FEET WHERE THOU AND I HENCEFORTH MAY NEVER MEET.
MY LORD, I DO PROTEST -

FOR THE LOVE OF GOD,
A SURGEON!
WHAT'S THE MATTER?
HE'S BROKE MY HEAD ACROSS,
AND SIR TOBY TOO.
WHO HAS DONE THIS?
THE COUNT'S GENTLEMAN, CESARIO.
HE'S THE VERY DEVIL INCARDINATE.

CESARIO?

YOU BROKE MY HEAD FOR NOTHING.

I WAS SET ON TO DO IT BY SIR TOBY.

WHY DO YOU SPEAK TO ME?

I NEVER HURT YOU.

NGG!

HOW IS IT WITH YOU?

WHOOP!

PATA
PATA
PATA
THAT'S ALL ONE.
HE'S HURT ME...
AND THERE'S THE END ON IT.
WHO HATH MADE THIS HAVOC WITH THEM?
I AM SORRY, MADAM, I HAVE HURT YOUR KINSMAN –
YOU THROW A STRANGE REGARD UPON ME...

PARDON ME, SWEET ONE, EVEN FOR THE VOWS WE MADE EACH OTHER BUT SO LATE AGO.
CHU
ONE FACE...
ONE VOICE...
ONE HABIT...
AND TWO PERSONS!
A NATURAL PERSPECTIVE, THAT IS AND IS NOT.
O MY DEAR ANTONIO!
HOW HAVE THE HOURS TORTURED ME SINCE I HAVE LOST THEE!
SEBASTIAN ARE YOU?

HOW HAVE YOU MADE DIVISION OF YOURSELF?
AN APPLE, CLEFT IN TWO, IS NOT MORE TWIN THAN THESE TWO CREATURES.
WHICH IS SEBASTIAN?
DAB
DAB
MOST WONDERFUL!

DO I STAND THERE?
I HAD A SISTER WHOM THE WAVES DEVOURED.
WHAT KIN ARE YOU TO ME?
WERE YOU A WOMAN, I SHOULD MY TEARS LET FALL UPON YOUR CHEEK AND SAY...
"THRICE WELCOME, DROWNED VIOLA!"

SEBASTIAN WAS MY BROTHER.
SO WENT HE TO HIS WATERY TOMB.
IF SPIRITS CAN ASSUME FORM, YOU COME TO FRIGHT US.
IF NOTHING LETS TO MAKE US HAPPY BUT THIS MY MASCULINE ATTIRE, DO NOT EMBRACE ME TILL I AM VIOLA...
WHICH TO CONFIRM, I'LL BRING YOU TO A CAPTAIN IN THIS TOWN BY WHOSE GENTLE HELP I WAS PRESERVED TO SERVE THIS NOBLE COUNT.

LADY, YOU HAVE BEEN MISTOOK.
YOU ARE BETROTHED BOTH TO A MAID AND MAN.
IF THIS BE SO, I SHALL HAVE SHARE IN THIS MOST HAPPY WRECK.
BOY, THOU HAST SAID TO ME A THOUSAND TIMES, THOU NEVER SHOULD LOVE WOMAN LIKE TO ME.
AND ALL THOSE SAYINGS WILL I KEEP AS TRUE.

GIVE ME THY HAND.
AND LET ME SEE THEE IN THY WOMAN'S WEEDS.
THE CAPTAIN THAT DID BRING ME ON SHORE HATH MY MAID'S GARMENTS.
HE, UPON SOME ACTION, IS NOW IN DURANCE AT MALVOLIO'S SUIT.
FETCH MALVOLIO HITHER.

ALAS, NOW I REMEMBER ME...
THEY SAY, POOR GENTLEMAN, HE'S MUCH DISTRACT.
MADAM, HE'S WRIT A LETTER TO YOU.
OPEN IT AND READ IT.
LOOK TO BE WELL EDIFIED WHEN THE FOOL DELIVERS THE MADMAN.
INHALE
EXHALE
UPSIDE-DOWN
? ?
SNATCH

"BY THE LORD, MADAM, YOU WRONG ME, AND THE WORLD SHALL KNOW IT."
"THOUGH YOU HAVE PUT ME INTO DARKNESS AND GIVEN YOUR DRUNKEN COUSIN RULE OVER ME, YET HAVE I THE BENEFIT OF MY SENSES AS WELL AS YOUR LADYSHIP.
I HAVE YOUR OWN LETTER THAT INDUCED ME TO THE SEMBLANCE I PUT ON..."
"THINK OF ME AS YOU PLEASE. I SPEAK OUT OF MY INJURY..."
"THE MADLY-USED MALVOLIO."

DID HE WRITE THIS?
RUSTLE
AY, MADAM.
RUSTLE
THIS SAVOURS NOT MUCH OF DISTRACTION.
SEE HIM DELIVERED, FABIAN.
BRING HIM HITHER.
MY LORD, SO PLEASE YOU, THINK ME AS WELL A SISTER AS A WIFE.
ONE DAY SHALL CROWN THE ALLIANCE HERE AT MY HOUSE, AND AT MY PROPER COST.
MADAM, I EMBRACE YOUR OFFER.

YOUR MASTER QUITS YOU FOR YOUR SERVICE DONE HIM.
HERE IS MY HAND.
YOU SHALL FROM THIS TIME BE YOUR MASTER'S MISTRESS.
A SISTER, YOU ARE SHE.

KLINK
IS THIS THE MADMAN?
AY, MY LORD, THIS SAME.
PATA
PATA
HOW NOW, MALVOLIO?

MADAM, YOU HAVE DONE ME WRONG,
NOTORIOUS WRONG.
HAVE I, MALVOLIO? NO.
LADY, YOU HAVE.
PRAY YOU PERUSE THAT LETTER.
TREMBLE
YOU MUST NOT NOW DENY IT IS YOUR HAND.
AND TELL ME WHY YOU BADE ME COME SMILING AND CROSS-GARTERED TO YOU?

TO PUT ON YELLOW STOCKINGS AND FROWN UPON SIR TOBY?
AND, ACTING THIS IN OBEDIENT HOPE, WHY HAVE YOU SUFFERED ME TO BE IMPRISONED IN A DARK HOUSE?
MADE THE MOST NOTORIOUS GULL THAT EVER INVENTION PLAYED ON?
TELL ME WHY!

ALAS, MALVOLIO...
THIS IS NOT MY WRITING...
THOUGH, I CONFESS, MUCH LIKE THE CHARACTER.
'TIS MARIA'S HAND.
BE CONTENT.
THOU SHALT BE BOTH THE PLAINTIFF AND THE JUDGE OF THINE OWN CAUSE.
LET NO QUARREL TAINT THE CONDITION OF THIS PRESENT HOUR.

MOST FREELY I CONFESS MYSELF AND TOBY SET THIS DEVICE AGAINST MALVOLIO.
10496
MARIA WRIT THE LETTER,
IN RECOMPENSE WHEREOF SIR TOBY HATH MARRIED HER.
10497
10498
SPORTFUL MALICE MAY RATHER PLUCK ON LAUGHTER THAN REVENGE.
ALAS, POOR FOOL! HOW HAVE THEY BAFFLED THEE!
WHY...
"SOME ARE BORN GREAT,
SOME ACHIEVE GREATNESS,
AND SOME HAVE GREATNESS THROWN UPON THEM"!

I WAS IN THIS INTERLUDE, SIR TOPAS, SIR –
"BY THE LORD, FOOL, I AM NOT MAD"!
BUT DO YOU REMEMBER?
"MADAM, WHY LAUGH YOU AT SUCH A BARREN RASCAL?"
DOFF
AND THUS THE WHIRLIGIG OF TIME BRINGS IN HIS REVENGES.
I'LL BE REVENGED ON THE WHOLE PACK OF YOU.

HE HATH BEEN MOST NOTORIOUSLY ABUSED.
PURSUE HIM, AND ENTREAT HIM TO A PEACE.
HE HATH NOT TOLD US OF THE CAPTAIN YET.
CESARIO, COME –
FOR SO YOU SHALL BE WHILE YOU ARE A MAN.
BUT WHEN IN OTHER HABITS YOU ARE SEEN...

ORSINO'S MISTRESS AND HIS FANCY'S QUEEN.
A GREAT WHILE AGO THE WORLD BEGUN, WITH HEY HO, THE WIND AND THE RAIN...
BUT THAT'S ALL ONE, OUR PLAY IS DONE, AND WE'LL STRIVE TO PLEASE YOU EVERY DAY.

PLOT SUMMARY OF TWELFTH NIGHT

The twins Viola and Sebastian, all but identical in appearance, are shipwrecked on the shores of Illyria, each thinking the other dead. Thrown upon her own resources, Viola disguises herself as a boy (calling herself Cesario) and presents herself for service at the court of Duke Orsino – with whom she promptly falls in love. But Orsino is carrying a torch for his neighbour, the Countess Olivia, who is in mourning for her dead brother and uninterested in Orsino's tiresome attentions. Living under Olivia's roof are two people who cordially detest each other: her uncle, the feckless alcoholic Sir Toby Belch; and her butler, the puritanical Malvolio, who is himself hopelessly smitten with her. Impressed by the qualities of "Cesario" (i.e. the disguised Viola), Orsino sends him/her as a go-between to Olivia's household, but his plan misfires: Viola/Cesario's eloquent pleading on his behalf leads to Olivia falling in love, not with Orsino, but with Viola/Cesario herself.

Meanwhile, Sir Toby has been cynically cultivating the friendship of a rich aristocrat, the cowardly Sir Andrew Aguecheek, falsely promising *him* the hand-in-marriage of his niece. With the help of three of Olivia's servants – the feisty maid Maria, the resourceful Fabian, and Feste her household jester – a plot is successfully hatched to engineer the downfall of the hated Malvolio by forging a letter to him from Olivia, in which she apparently declares her love for him: when Malvolio acts on this letter, dressing in an incongruously flamboyant style and grinning at Olivia, he is declared mad.

This whirlwind of unrequited love is at last resolved by the appearance of Viola's "lost" twin, Sebastian, who, immediately falling in love with Olivia, prompts a series of misunderstandings and quarrels. Following the twins' joyful reunion, both Viola and Orsino, and Sebastian and Olivia, are free to declare their love – but others are left out in the cold. Sir Toby violently falls out with the cowardly Sir Andrew, who leaves for home after a farcical duel with Viola and a more violent offstage encounter with Sebastian; Antonio, the sea-captain who has adoringly steered Sebastian to this outcome, is now abandoned; Malvolio is released from his confinement, but vows revenge; and Feste the fool is left alone to sing the last of his sad songs.

A BRIEF LIFE OF WILLIAM SHAKESPEARE

Shakespeare's birthday is traditionally said to be the 23rd of April – St George's Day, patron saint of England. A good start for England's greatest writer. But that date and even his name are uncertain. He signed his own name in different ways. "Shakespeare" is now the accepted one out of dozens of different versions.

He was born at Stratford-upon-Avon in 1564, and baptized on 26th April. His mother, Mary Arden, was the daughter of a prosperous farmer. His father, John Shakespeare, a glove-maker, was a respected civic figure – and probably also a Catholic. In 1570, just as Will began school, his father was accused of illegal dealings. The family fell into debt and disrepute.

Will attended a local school for eight years. He did not go to university. The next ten years are a blank filled by suppositions. Was he briefly a Latin teacher, a soldier, a sea-faring explorer? Was he prosecuted and whipped for poaching deer?

We do know that in 1582 he married Anne Hathaway, eight years his senior, and three months pregnant. Two more children – twins – were born three years later but, by around 1590, Will had left Stratford to pursue a theatre career in London. Shakespeare's apprenticeship began as an actor and "pen for hire".

He learned his craft the hard way. He soon won fame as a playwright with often-staged popular hits.

He and his colleagues formed a stage company, the Lord Chamberlain's Men, which built the famous Globe Theatre. It opened in 1599 but was destroyed by fire in 1613 during a performance of *Henry VIII* which used gunpowder special effects. It was rebuilt in brick the following year.

Shakespeare was a financially successful writer who invested his money wisely in property. In 1597, he bought an enormous house in Stratford, and in 1608 became a shareholder in London's Blackfriars Theatre. He also redeemed the family's honour by acquiring a personal coat of arms.

Shakespeare wrote over 40 works, including poems, "lost" plays and collaborations, in a career spanning nearly 25 years. He retired to Stratford in 1613, where he died on 23rd April 1616, aged 52, apparently of a fever after a "merry meeting" of drinks with friends. Shakespeare did in fact die on St George's Day! He was buried "full 17 foot deep" in Holy Trinity Church, Stratford, and left an epitaph cursing anyone who dared disturb his bones.

There have been preposterous theories disputing Shakespeare's authorship. Some claim that Sir Francis Bacon (1561–1626), philosopher and Lord Chancellor, was the real author of Shakespeare's plays. Others propose Edward de Vere, Earl of Oxford (1550–1604), or, even more weirdly, Queen Elizabeth I. The implication is that the "real" Shakespeare had to be a university graduate or an aristocrat. Nothing less would do for the world's greatest writer.

Shakespeare is mysteriously hidden behind his work. His life will not tell us what inspired his genius.